D0819617

SEVEN GOLDEN RINGS

A Tale of Music and Math

by Rajani LaRocca

illustrated by Archana Sreenivasan

Lee & Low Books Inc.
New York

Text copyright © 2020 by Rajani LaRocca

Illustrations copyright © 2020 by Archana Sreenivasan

All rights reserved. No part of this book may be reproduced, transmitted, or stored in
an information retrieval system in any form or by any means, electronic, mechanical,
photocopying, recording, or otherwise, without written permission from the publisher.

LEE & LOW BOOKS Inc., 95 Madison Avenue, New York, NY 10016

leeandlow.com

Edited by Cheryl Klein | Book design by Rachel Eeva Wood | Book production by The Kids at Our House
The text is set in Aria Text G2, with the display type in Alice and handlettering by Archana Sreenivasan.
The illustrations were created digitally.
Manufactured in China by Jade Productions
Printed on paper from responsible sources
10 9 8 7 6 5 4 3 2 1
First Edition

Library of Congress Cataloging-in-Publication Data
Names: LaRocca, Rajani, author. | Sreenivasan, Archana, illustrator.
Title: Seven golden rings : a tale of music and math / by Rajani LaRocca ; illustrated by Archana Sreenivasan.
Description: First edition. | New York : Lee & Low Books Inc., [2020] | Audience: Ages 7-10. | Audience: Grades 2-3. |
Summary: In ancient India, a boy named Bhagat travels to the rajah's city, hoping to ensure his family's prosperity
by winning a place at court as a singer. Includes author's note about binary numbers.
Identifiers: LCCN 2020007425 | ISBN 9781885008978 (hardcover)
Subjects: CYAC: Problem solving--Fiction. | Mathematics--Fiction. | Singing--Fiction. | India--History--Fiction.
Classification: LCC PZ7.1.L353 Se 2020 | DDC [E]--dc23
LC record available at https://lccn.loc.gov/2020007425

For Joe, who has loved music and math from the very start —*R.L.*

←-→

For my father—who tried very hard to instill in us his love for math —*A.S.*

Long ago there lived a kind rajah who ruled over vast lands. He loved music, and gathered the finest players and singers to perform in his court. But the rajah had no interest in planning or calculating, and did not manage his kingdom's food stores and accounts. And so his people suffered.

Bhagat and his mother lived in a dusty village in the far corner of the rajah's kingdom. Their days were filled with toil and hunger, but they planned and saved to make their meager means stretch further.

And Bhagat, who loved to sing,
filled their nights with song.

One day, Bhagat saw something that gave him hope.

For one week only, the Rajah calls on musicians to audition for the royal troupe.

"Amma, we'll soon starve. I must seek our fortune and win a place with the rajah."

"You are still young," said Bhagat's mother, "and only the most skilled musicians will be chosen for the rajah's troupe. The journey will be long. And what will happen if you fail?"

But Bhagat would not change his mind. "This is our only chance. I must win the rajah's favor with my singing."

Eventually, Bhagat's mother relented. She gave him one rupee, the last they had, and a chain of seven tiny golden rings.

"This is what remains of my wedding necklace. I have sold it ring by ring so we could eat. Use it to change our fortune. Remember, Bhagat, you are a fine singer. But you are an even finer thinker. Consider all you have to offer the rajah."

And she gave Bhagat her blessing.

Bhagat sang as he walked all day.
In his head, he heard a rhythm:
of whole notes—*Taan*,
and half notes—*Thaa Thaa*,
and quarter notes—*Tha-ka Tha-ka*.
So many ways to divide a whole!
As long as he had music,
Bhagat never felt alone.

He reached the city and found a
small inn.

"Ten rupees a night, including
dinner," said the innkeeper.

But Bhagat had only one rupee.
"Sir, may I work for my stay?"

"I'm sorry, no."

Bhagat revealed the seven golden rings. They glimmered in the twilight.

"Seven rings for seven nights. Hand them over," said the innkeeper's wife.

But Bhagat didn't know how many nights he would remain in the city. If the rajah called him the next day, he would have spent all seven rings when he only needed one.

"Madam, may I pay when I leave, and only for the days I stayed?"

"You must pay for each night in advance—one ring per night. Divide them if you must," she said, flinging her sari over her shoulder.

"There is a goldsmith nearby," whispered the innkeeper.

"I can separate them all for five rupees," said the goldsmith.

"But I only have one."

"One rupee, one link broken."

Bhagat thought and thought. If he broke the first link, he would have a single ring and a chain of six. That would work for one night, but what would he do if the rajah didn't call him the next day? He would need to give up the rest of the necklace when perhaps only one more ring would do.

Maybe he should break the second link. With some wiggling he could free it from the first, and he would have two single rings and a chain of five. But if he needed to stay more than two nights, he would have to give the innkeeper all the remaining rings.

Bhagat was determined not to waste a single precious ring of his mother's wedding necklace. How could he pay the innkeeper one ring each night if he couldn't separate them all?

Bhagat wandered the city.

Remember, Bhagat, you are a thinker.

He heard the rhythm in his head:

Taan, Thaa Thaa, Tha-ka Tha-ka.

So many ways to divide a whole.

Suddenly, he knew
what to do!

He raced back and
had the goldsmith
break the third link.

Seven golden rings became
one ring by itself,
a chain of two, and
a chain of four.

Bhagat gave the innkeeper the single ring and begged him not to sell it right away.

The next day, he waited at the palace, but was not called.

That night, he asked for the single ring back, and handed over the chain of two.

Each morning, Bhagat went to the palace. He
waited and thought of his mother, alone and hungry.
Each evening, he returned to the inn.

On the third night, Bhagat gave the innkeeper the single ring to join the two.

On the fourth night, he took three rings back and gave him the chain of four.

On the fifth night, he gave him the single ring to join the four.

On the sixth, he took back the single and handed over the chain of two.

On the seventh night, Bhagat gave up the last golden ring.

"This was all that Amma and I had left."

"May God give you luck with the rajah tomorrow."

As the sun sank on the final day,
Bhagat was called to sing at last.

He sang of parched land quenched
by cooling rains, long journeys on
tired feet, and the love of a family,
more precious than gold.

"You are good, but not polished enough," said the rajah. "Return next year."

Bhagat had risked everything, and now he had nothing.

"O Rajah, do not let him go!" cried a voice from the crowd.

It was the innkeeper's wife. "He may not sing to your liking, but this young man can think. He devised a plan to divide his necklace into a single ring, a chain of two, and a chain of four, then combined them in just the right ways to ensure he never overpaid for his room. O Rajah, he may be just the person to help run your estates."

"Ah," said the rajah. "Do I need such a person?"

"My Rajah," said Bhagat. "As this honorable woman has said, I came here with only seven golden rings, but because I planned and calculated, I was able to avoid wasting even one. I have experience in making the smallest treasures last as long as possible. It would be the highest honor to help you do the same for our people."

"Impressive thinking," said the rajah. "Bhagat, will you stay?"

Bhagat arrived home at dusk the next day.

"Amma! Our fortune has changed!"

"So you are the rajah's singer!"

"No, Amma, you were right. I will be the rajah's thinker."

From then on, Bhagat and his mother lived at the palace. Bhagat planned and saved so all the rajah's people prospered. Their days were filled with hard work and abundance.

And Bhagat filled their nights with song.

W_HEN WE FIRST LEARN ABOUT NUMBERS AND COUNTING, we use a system called *base ten*, or *decimal*. Every number is expressed by a series of digits, and the position of each digit within the number is called its *place*. In base ten, there are ten possible values for each digit—0 through 9—and each additional place in the number increases by a *power of ten*. Here's an example:

$$2,059$$

2 thousands + 0 hundreds + 5 tens + 9 ones = 2,059
2,000   0   50   9

The digit 9, in the ones place, tells us there are nine ones in the number. The 5 to its left, in the tens place, tells us there are five tens in the number (five times ten times one, or 50). The 0 tells us how many hundreds (zero times ten times ten, or 0), and the 2, thousands (two times ten times ten times ten, or 2000). And of course, 2000 + 0 + 50 + 9 = 2,059. If we wanted to create a bigger number, we could use a ten thousands place (ten times ten times ten times ten), a hundred thousands place (ten times ten times ten times ten times ten), and on and on.

But there are other ways of thinking about numbers, including *base two*, or *binary*. In binary, the place farthest to the right is still the ones place, but the place to its left is the twos (two times one), the third from the right is the fours (two times two), the fourth is the eights (two times two times two), and on and on in *powers of two*. Moreover, binary allows only two possible values for each digit: 0 or 1. A 1 in a certain place indicates that place is added toward the final number. Thus, the decimal number 2 is written as *10* in base two, with a 1 in the twos place and no ones (2 + 0 = 2). Three in base two is written as *11,* with a 1 in the twos place and a 1 in the ones place (2 + 1 = 3). Four is *100*, with a 1 in the fours place, no twos, and no ones (4 + 0 + 0 = 4); five is *101*, with 1 in the fours place, no twos, and 1 in the ones place (4 + 0 + 1 = 5).

By creating additional places—multiplying the value of the previous place by two each time—we can write any decimal number we want in binary, using only the digits 0 and 1. Here's the number 21:

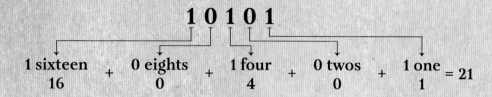

$$1 \times 16 + 0 \times 8 + 1 \times 4 + 0 \times 2 + 1 \times 1 = 21$$

The sixteens, fours, and ones digits are all 1, so the numbers sixteen, four, and one are counted toward the total (16 + 4 + 1 = 21). Since the eights and twos digits are both 0s, they are not counted. Can you figure out how to write eight in binary? How about ten? How about twenty-seven?

We can think of Bhagat's sets of rings as each representing a different binary digit—the single ring representing a 1 in the ones place, the chain with two rings representing a 1 in the twos place, and the chain with four rings representing a 1 in the fours place. Bhagat was able to use those three chains to create every number up to seven. If he had a fourth chain with eight rings, he could have gone all the way up to fifteen!

Decimal	Binary	Rings
1	1	the single ring, or *one one*
2	10	the chain of two alone, or *one two, no ones*
3	11	the chain of two and the single ring, or *one two, one one*
4	100	the chain of four alone, or *one four, no twos, no ones*
5	101	the chain of four and the single ring, or *one four, no twos, one one*
6	110	the chain of four and the chain of two, or *one four, one two, no ones*
7	111	the chain of four, the chain of two, and the single ring, or *one four, one two, one one*

Bhagat's story is fictional, but people have used both the binary and decimal number systems for centuries. There is evidence of ancient cultures in China and India using binary as early as the ninth to the second centuries BCE, although the modern form of binary was invented by the German mathematician Gottfried Wilhelm Leibniz in the 1600s. Decimal, also known as the *Hindu-Arabic number system*, is thought to have originated in India in the fifth century CE.

The decimal system is the easiest way for people to count, because we have ten fingers. But it turns out that the best way for computers to count is binary. Why is that? Computers, smartphones, and other electronic devices rely on electric signals for everything they do, and electric signals have just two modes: on or off. You can think of a binary number as a row of lightbulbs, with each bulb representing a place in the number. Every bulb that's switched on is a 1, and every bulb that's off is a 0. What base-ten number is represented here?

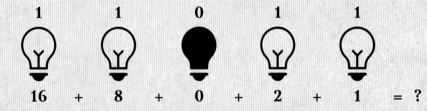

Computer scientists use the word *bit*, short for **b**inary dig**it**, to describe each of the zeroes and ones that flow through a computer's circuits. Eight bits are called a *byte*—enough room to encode any number from 0 to 255 (that's two to the eighth power, or two times two times two times two times two times two times two times two, which equals 256 different values if you include 0). One thousand bytes are called a *kilobyte*, one million bytes are a *megabyte*, and one billion bytes are called a *gigabyte*. The amount of information computers can hold keeps growing and growing, so we have to keep inventing new words to count it: *terabyte*, *petabyte*, *exabyte*, and so on!

Every piece of information, or data, on a computer—the music you listen to, the games you play, or the movies you watch—is encoded using binary numbers. When I wrote this book, it used about fifty kilobytes of data on my computer. Your favorite song might use four or five megabytes of data, while a two-hour movie might use three gigabytes or more. That's billions and billions of zeroes and ones being counted at lightning speed according to the same rules Bhagat used to pay the innkeeper with his seven golden rings!